Molly's New Pony, Sir Wallace McGee

A Story of Courage to Be All You Can Be!

David Casentini

AuthorHouse™
1663 Liberty Drive
Bloomington, IN 47403
www.authorhouse.com
Phone: 833-262-8899

Because of the dynamic nature of the Internet, any web addresses or links contained in this book may have changed since publication and may no longer be valid. The views expressed in this work are solely those of the author and do not necessarily reflect the views of the publisher, and the publisher hereby disclaims any responsibility for them.

Any people depicted in stock imagery provided by Getty Images are models, and such images are being used for illustrative purposes only.
Certain stock imagery © Getty Images.

This book is printed on acid-free paper.

ISBN: 979-8-8230-0856-3 (sc)
ISBN: 979-8-8230-0875-4 (hc)
ISBN: 979-8-8230-0857-0 (e)

Library of Congress Control Number: 2023909601

Print information available on the last page.

Published by AuthorHouse 05/23/2023

authorHOUSE

Dedication

To my wife Lauren, our children Bianca, Jason, Renèe and Elisa, and our grandchildren Chloe, Mila, Conor and Aubrey, for giving me the opportunity to be more than I thought possible. Special thanks to Alex Stanton for his illustrative inspiration and support.

"Yippee! Hurray!" Molly did say on the eleventh day of May, a very special birthday.

Her parents told her this day would come...

with ribbons, balloons and truckloads of fun!

On the grass by the barn at the back of their home lay
a newborn little pony she could now call her own!

So frail and small, gentle and sweet,
his long legs wobbled as he rose to his feet.

"You're the best horse of all!" cried Molly with
glee, "and you I shall name Sir Wallace McGee!"

Her friends all did laugh at the sound of his name,
but her parents soon said, "Name him just the same."

They said, "Grandma Wallace will be proud that he is named after her and Aunt Millie McGee!"

Other horses on the ranch looked at Wallace and said,
"That pony doesn't stand a chance
against us thoroughbreds."

And the horses went to play
in a field all their own

while Wallace felt different,
ashamed, and alone.

Molly remembered those feelings so well,
those feelings that aren't so easy to tell.

Not sure of yourself
or the things you can do,

or the support you need
that will make a difference for you.

So Molly soon whispered
in Wallace's ear

these words from her parents
that she used to hear:

"You're loved, you're unique;
Reach far and run free.
Be all the things you dream you can be!"

There are horses that race

or place first at horse shows...

Horses that carry loads when heavy winds blow.

Horses that march in a great, grand parade...

And horses that fill dreams
where wishes are made.

"Whatever you choose, work hard to succeed.
I'll always love you because you matter to me!"

He slowly grew taller and stronger but still
felt other horses were much better until
he thought of a plan where he could show he was worthy.

He would race against horses
in Springtown's annual derby!

Molly thought the plan was a little bit much
but thought maybe, just maybe,
with hard work and some luck

Wallace's chance to race with the best
could help him shine above the rest.

Two months and three days of hard work and little play turned Wallace's dream from bright to gray.

"This task is too great!" thought Wallace at last.
"I won't ever be good enough, strong enough, or fast."

So Molly repeated the words she held dear,
whispering to Wallace calmly and clear:

His brave heart was pounding, his nerves all a-flutter,
"I know I can do this!" they heard him mutter.

"This task is too great!" thought Wallace at last.
"I won't ever be good enough, strong enough, or fast."

So Molly repeated the words she held dear,
whispering to Wallace calmly and clear:

"You're loved, you're unique;
Reach far and run free.
Be all the things you dream you can be!"

Wallace continued to work harder and harder
until he was running much faster and farther.

His confidence grew and his dream burned bright.
It seemed nothing could stop him,
his will, or his might.

And soon, race day was here
and not a moment too late.
Wallace stood firm at the starting gate.

His brave heart was pounding, his nerves all a-flutter,
"I know I can do this!" they heard him mutter.

"Briiinnnggg!" went the bell, and the gates flew open
but Wallace paused slightly, his spirit broken.

The other horses sped quickly away
while Wallace's hopes were starting to fade.

But the words from Molly
and her parents rang clear.

They lifted his spirits
and put him in high gear:

"You're loved, you're unique;
Reach far and run free.
Be all the things you dream you can be!"

And with that, he shot from the gate with such force, like a fast-moving train, not just a young horse!

And soon, he caught up to the pack just ahead and started to pass the grand thoroughbreds! Around the last turn, he looked up and could see the finish line fast approaching, so he

ran even harder and faster until he finished the race, exhausted and thrilled!

Though he didn't come in first,
second or third,

he reached his goal
and kept his word.

To race against others
and prove that he would

reach higher, dream bigger
than he thought he could.

Molly and her family proudly embraced
this sweet little horse who ran his first race.

As the sun set and day turned to night, those words that
were spoken came through clear and bright:

"You're loved, you're unique;
Reach far and run free.
Be all the things you dream you can be!"

Molly and Wallace want you to remember:
There is only one YOU, and you make a difference!
Because you are unique, you can live life your way...
Dream big and achieve goals that matter to you.
You are a gift to the world, and the love and support
that you bring to those around you
make a difference in their lives and yours.

Ingram Content Group UK Ltd.
Milton Keynes UK
UKHW050622080623
422968UK00003B/115